As members of the
MAGIC ATTIC CLUB,
we promise to
be best friends,
share all of our adventures in the attic,
use our imaginations,
have lots of fun together,
and remember—the real magic is in us.

Alison   Keisha

Heather   Megan

Contents

DOWNHILL MEGAN
by Trisha Magraw

Illustrations by
Janîce Leotti

Spot Illustrations by
Rich Grote

MAGIC ATTIC PRESS

Published by Magic Attic Press.

For more information contact:
Book Editor, Magic Attic Press, 866 Spring Street,
P.O. Box 9722, Portland, ME 04104-5022.

First Edition
Printed in the United States of America
1 2 3 4 5 6 7 8 9 10

Betsy Gould, Editorial Director
Marva Martin, Art Director
Robin Haywood, Managing Editor

Edited by Judit Bodnar
Designed by Susi Oberhelman

ISBN 1-57513-023-8

Magic Attic Club books are printed on acid-free, recycled paper.

Chapter

One

SPRING
VACATION

Megan was surprised when her three best friends—
Keisha Vance, Heather Hardin, and Alison
McCann—burst unexpectedly through her bedroom door.
Megan had been deep in thought, trying to decide what
to pack for spring vacation. When she said good-bye to
her friends after school that day, she hadn't expected to
see them again until it was time to go back to school.

"This is a going-away present from all three of us.
Here," said Alison, handing Megan three books tied with

a big bow of blue yarn. "We hear the airline attendants give all the kids on the plane crossword-puzzle books to keep them busy, but we wanted you to have these."

Megan was packing for a ski vacation with her father, a foreign correspondent who was covering a story in Switzerland. He had arranged for Megan to fly over for a whole week so they could be together and learn how to ski in the Swiss Alps.

Megan untied the bow and tossed it to Ginger, who was napping in a suitcase on the floor. Soon the playful cat was rolling around the floor with her new toy.

"This is perfect!" cried Megan, looking at the first book. It was a collection of funny short stories about cats.

"Lucky duck!" said Alison. "Going on a plane all the way to Switzerland." Of the four girls, Alison was the one who had flown the most. Sometimes Alison flew to Florida to visit her grandparents over spring vacation. But this year she was needed at home, helping out while painters put a fresh coat of paint on the whole second floor of her house. Megan had helped Alison pick a soft blue for her bedroom, and she almost wished she could be around to see how it changed the old white room.

"Get to the next one," urged Keisha who was going away with her family on their first camping trip of the season.

"A mystery!" cried Megan, pulling off the wrapping paper. She couldn't get enough of Agatha Christie and Nancy Drew, or almost any mystery series for that matter. Mysteries were the best books when you were traveling and wanted the time to go fast. "*The Great Ski Robbery*. And it takes place at a ski resort, too. How did you know I haven't read this one?"

"A good guess," said Keisha. "Second-Chance Books had a lot of mysteries. We figured this one was right for the occasion."

Second-Chance Books was the secondhand bookstore in town where Megan spent her allowance money to buy books practically every month. Her shelves were jammed with new and used books, paperback and hardcover, and she had read them all.

"Okay, now for the really important book," declared Heather when Megan got to the last one in the pile. It was a French-English/English-French dictionary. There was also a section at the beginning called "Useful French Phrases."

"*Oui*," said Megan, then "*Merci*," as she put on a thick French accent that didn't sound bad at all. "Thanks. I'm going to keep this one with me at all times, since I don't know a word of French."

"You seem to know two words," kidded Heather.

"You're so lucky that your dad travels to such great places," said Alison.

"Yeah," said Megan, but her heart clearly wasn't in it. She watched as her friends talked excitedly together, helping fold her clothes and making sure she  remembered to pack the new camera that her mother had gotten for her.

"And don't forget your thermal underwear. I hear it's really cold over there," said Keisha, placing a pair of long johns and a heavy undershirt in the bottom of Megan's suitcase.

"Are you flying all by yourself?" Alison wanted to know.

"Yes and no," replied Megan. "I mean, Dad's worked it out so one of his business friends is taking the same flight to Paris with his wife. Then they'll make sure I get on the right smaller plane to the ski resort, but I've never met them before, so it's a lot like flying alone."

"I wonder how close you fly to the mountaintops," said Keisha. "Sometimes those little planes fly really low. I wonder if it will be like the travel movies, where you feel like you're right there. It'll be great."

Megan had never flown without her parents before, and gulped hard. She envied Keisha's sense of adventure.

When it was time for her friends to go home, Megan hugged each one of them, feeling sad. Then she stood at her bedroom window waving good-bye until they turned the corner and disappeared from sight.

Megan was happy about having a whole week with her father. They had talked for months about spending a long vacation together, not just a weekend visit. She and her father liked to do a lot of the same things and Megan knew she wouldn't be bored for one minute. Still, her friends seemed more excited about a ski vacation in Europe than she was.

Megan felt a warm ball of fur bounce against her foot. Poor Ginger had managed to get herself all tangled up in the yarn. "Silly thing," Megan told the cat, untwisting a mittenlike paw from the jumble. "What in the world will you do without me?"

Megan's diary was lying on the bed. It was open to a brand-new page, all blank and waiting for her.

Dear Diary, Megan began. *Maybe my friends should be going on this*

vacation instead of me! They sure seem a lot more excited. I keep thinking about the things I have to do right here. I know that sounds silly, but I've got a big assignment due the day I get back. Plus Mom's having a lot of dental work done, and she might need me to help her out if she feels bad. Aunt Frances is going away, too, so Mom will be here all alone. . . .

Soon the pages were damp with tears. Megan wiped her hand across the page, smudging several words. Then she began to cry into her pillow.

"What in the world is wrong?" Megan could hear the concern in her mother's voice as she stood in the doorway. Then Megan felt a cool hand on her head. When something was wrong, her mother usually checked Megan's forehead first for a fever, as though that would tell the whole story.

"I don't think I'm sick," replied Megan, wiping away her tears with the lacy edge of her pillowcase. "I just wish you were coming with us, that's all."

Megan's mother gave her a big hug. "I don't think that's really what's wrong, but I'm glad to know I'll be missed."

Megan cracked a little smile.

"Now," her mother began in a cheerful way, "let's figure out what's really upsetting you."

Chapter

Two

COLD FEET

ell, maybe I *am* coming down with something,"
Megan began.

"You may be coming down with cold feet," her mother
replied.

"I wish I knew how to ski," Megan blurted out. "I'm
going to spend the whole vacation sitting in the snow!"

"Well, your father may be sitting there with you," joked
her mother. "Have you forgotten that he's a beginner, too?
I think the ski term for the two of you is *snow bunnies*."

Megan began to smile. "Then maybe the snow bunnies will make snow angels together, the way we used to when I was little and the snow had just fallen in the yard," she said. Just that thought made Megan feel a little bit better. Then she remembered she'd be taking two airplanes the very next day. "Remember how I sat between you and Dad when we flew to Disney World, and I had about ten glasses of apple juice?"

"And your father got to take you to the bathroom about ten times because he was on the aisle." They laughed together at the memory.

"I guess I'm a little worried about flying alone. Well, not alone, because Dad's friends will be there, but I don't really know them." Megan sighed loudly.

"You'll do just fine," Her mother's voice sounded comforting as she folded a pair of flannel pajamas and placed them in the suitcase. "Hasn't Alison flown alone once or twice?"

"Yes, but she hasn't ever had to change planes. What if I get lost at the Paris airport, looking for the plane to the resort?"

"The Jamisons will see to it that you don't."

"I guess," said Megan. "I just hope Dad remembers to meet my plane. I wouldn't even be able to tell somebody that I'm lost if they didn't speak English."

"I guarantee that your father will be there at the gate. Early." Megan's mother picked up the new dictionary and began to thumb through it. Then she tossed it to Megan. "Look up *courage*."

Megan turned to the C's. "*Courage*," Megan read out loud. "Hey, it's the same word in French and in English!"

"And I know you have plenty of courage, no matter what language you're speaking."

Megan wrapped her arms around her mother's neck, and her mother hugged her back.

"I'll finish the packing," her mother said. "I imagine there are a few things you need to do before bedtime."

"You're terrific," Megan said, giving her mother a loud kiss on the cheek. "Thanks."

Her mother was right about Megan still having things to do. There was one thing she could think of right away, and that was to say good-bye to Ellie.

Megan grabbed her jacket. As she headed down the block, a million things danced around in her head. She needed time for her thoughts to settle. She needed a place to think. All of a sudden, Megan knew what she really wanted to do. After she talked to Ellie, she'd go upstairs to the attic. There was just enough time.

Megan found Ellie pasting postcards in a big album. "I've been meaning to organize these for years," Ellie said with a sigh, pleased with her progress.

The big dining room table was covered with postcards from all over the world. Ellie had organized them by year. Right on top of one pile, Megan spotted one of a snow-covered mountain range. She wondered if that was what the Swiss Alps were going to look like.

"I hope you'll have time to send me a card," said Ellie. "You must be very excited."

"Sort of," replied Megan.

"Oh, I know all about travel," said Ellie, whose career in

the theater had taken her to many foreign places. "It's hard to feel ready for a big trip like yours."

"My suitcase is almost ready," Megan sighed. "But I'm not sure I am."

"I understand," replied Ellie, looking at the photograph of the snow-peaked mountains on the card. "But when you get there and realize how much there is to see and do—that's what makes the effort worthwhile. All your hesitations will disappear."

"Is it like going on a trip through the mirror?" asked Megan.

"Why not go find out, my dear?" Ellie waved in the direction of the hallway and the key to the attic. "Don't waste another minute down here."

As soon as Megan had the golden key in her hand, she hurried up the two flights of stairs and gazed around the attic. She loved the wonderful outfits that Ellie had collected over the years. And of course, she loved the amazing adventures to other times and places that she and Alison, Keisha, and Heather had taken when they tried the outfits on in front of the gilt-edged mirror.

Megan almost tripped over a thick photo album as she walked over to the steamer trunk. A few old photos spilled across the floor. Megan noticed the faded images of people from another time playing tennis and croquet, women having tea in long white dresses, and families taking drives in cars that looked like gigantic tin boxes with doors and a roof. Quickly, she tucked the photos back into the album.

Megan opened the trunk and discovered a brightly-colored bathing suit folded neatly on top. Right under the bathing suit was a smart-looking tennis outfit trimmed in red, white, and blue.

"I must have sports on my mind," she said out loud when she discovered a gold ski parka that glowed like a bright moon, as well as jet-black pants that set it off perfectly. When Megan looked further, she found a fuzzy magenta-colored sweater and furry black ski mittens.

"Gorgeous!" cried Megan as she slipped the sweater over her head and put on the parka. Its furry trim tickled as she pulled the hood up and tucked her strawberry blond hair inside. The mittens felt cozy and warm.

A pair of sleek black skis decorated with glittery, multicolored stars stood in the corner. Beside them was a pair of bright fuschia ski poles. After a bit of searching, Megan found black ski boots just her size behind a stack of old quilts and quickly sat down to put them on.

Holding the poles in her hands, Megan stood in front of the long mirror and slowly bent her knees. "I guess I'm going skiing somewhere," she whispered to herself. "I just wish I knew *how* to ski." She rubbed the soft, furry cuffs of her mittens against her cheeks. "Well, at least I won't *look* like a snow bunny."

At that moment, Megan felt herself sliding. A cold wind ruffled her hair as she caught her balance.

"Zip up," someone cried, "or you'll freeze on your way down."

Megan looked around. The scene was just like the picture of the Alps on Ellie's postcard. She was surrounded by peak after peak of incredibly beautiful snow-covered mountains. They rose higher than any she had ever imagined.

In the distance, Megan saw a girl about her age wearing a red parka and ski pants to match. The big tassel on the girl's ski hat bobbed in the wind as she motioned to Megan to follow her.

Megan stared at the snow beneath her skis and at the steep slope ahead of her. She swallowed hard as she zipped the parka all the way to her chin. "Here I come!" she cried, giving a small push with her poles. Inside the mittens, her fingers were crossed on both hands.

Chapter
Three

READY OR NOT

The cold, fresh air in her face filled Megan with energy. She rounded a curve with surprising speed. Pleased with her unexpected skill, she pushed her pace a little harder, laughing when she thought of her fears about falling and sliding uncontrollably down the slope. That was Snow Bunny Megan. Now she was Megan the Hot Dog, ready to show off!

She quickly caught up to the girl in the red ski outfit and passed her.

"Hey, wait for me," cried the girl. At the fork in the trail, Megan waited for her to catch up. "Maybe we shouldn't have decided to ski together. You must have been born on skis," the girl said breathlessly.

"You might say that," Megan replied. That wasn't a yes and it wasn't a no. After all, she didn't know yet who anybody was in this adventure. As Megan bent down to check her bindings, she noticed that LIZZIE ROBINSON was printed on the girl's skis and she introduced herself to her new friend.

Behind her, the clouds over the mountain had turned gray and mean-looking. The wind whipped around her ears and small crystals of snow blew into her eyes. "We'd better take off," she told Lizzie, knowing that Lizzie would need a little extra time.

Lizzie and Megan took the shortest way down. It was also one of the most difficult, but the loose powder under Megan's skis felt good. She leaned into the hill as she quickly turned once, then again and again, with her skis close together, the way she had read that experts skied. Every once in a while, Megan looked back to make sure Lizzie was okay. Lizzie had to work a little harder at keeping her balance, but she was a good skier. Daring, too.

When the two girls got to the bottom of the mountain, it was just starting to snow there. It was funny the way ski

24

conditions could change so quickly and without much warning. Both the chairlift and the gondola were closed now because of the approaching storm. It might have been dangerous to stay out any longer.

"This calls for hot chocolate—my favorite whenever we ski in the Alps. My treat," declared Lizzie, wiping the snow from her goggles.

So that's where I am! thought Megan. "Lead the way," she replied. Megan was glad to get to know Lizzie better. She liked her cheerful and friendly personality and the way Lizzie hadn't hesitated to take a trail that was sure to be a challenge. Megan was eager to learn more about her.

As they walked through the village to the big mountainside lodge that overlooked it, Megan couldn't tell who was an American and who wasn't. Everybody was bundled up in ski caps, scarves, and heavy parkas.

"*Excusez moi*," said Megan in her best French when she accidently bumped a woman with her skis.

"Oh, that's okay, honey," replied the woman in clear English. They both laughed.

"I wish I spoke French," moaned Lizzie. "All the words I do know come from menus. Yesterday when my parents and I arrived, the man at the front desk said '*Bonjour*,' and I just stood there with my mouth open. Nothing came out and I felt silly."

"My French is pretty bad, too," admitted Megan, hoping that Lizzie wouldn't find out just how bad it was.

The village looked like something that belonged in the middle of a tiny train set under a Christmas tree. It was as though time had stopped, or at least slowed down. The shops and restaurants were cottages, their roofs covered with snow. The sidewalks were narrow, and people walked in the cobblestone streets. Small European cars, all with ski racks on their roofs, moved along at a snail's pace. Even with the crowd of noisy skiers, Megan could hear the old town clock clearly as it announced the hour. Glass chimes tinkled in the doorway of one of the stores as they passed.

At a little round table in the lobby of the lodge, Lizzie and Megan sipped their steaming drinks.

"I can't believe how cold I was," declared Megan, rubbing her red fingers. "This hot chocolate was a great idea. Thanks."

"Swiss and German chocolate are the best," said Lizzie. "My dad said that's why he came to the Swiss

Alps—for the chocolate!"

"Do both your parents ski?"
Megan wanted to know.

"Yes, when they have time,"
Lizzie said with a little moan. "I
mean, my parents decided this
time to combine business and
pleasure. They're antiques
dealers who specialize in rare
European objects, like porcelain
vases that are hundreds of years old
and candleholders that once belonged to royalty. You
know, that sort of thing."

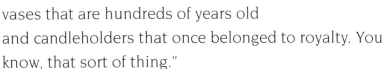

"I'll bet your home is beautiful," cried Megan.

"Oh, we don't live that way," laughed Lizzie. "We have
a regular house with a dog that jumps up on the sofa."

"Like us," responded Megan, "only at our house it's
Ginger, my cat. What kind of business do your parents
have at a ski resort?" Megan wanted to know. It seemed
like a strange place to come to buy and sell antiques.

"They came to Switzerland to buy a jeweled box from
an old baroness. She happens to live in a castle in the
mountains nearby. My parents drove out to see her after
we checked in. They're supposed to buy the box and bring
it back. That's why I was skiing alone before I met you."

"I have a jewelry box covered with pretty fabric that my father gave me for Christmas last year," commented Megan, trying to picture the one Lizzie was talking about.

Lizzie smiled. "It might be the same size," she said, "but the jewels on this box are rare, especially the blue ice diamond on top."

"It sounds incredible. And expensive," said Megan.

"Oh, it is," Lizzie replied. "But you can't really put a price on it. There's only one like it, and that's much more important than money. The story behind it is what makes it really special, though. Supposedly the box was Alexander the Great's talisman—you know, it was thought to bring him good fortune. That's why it's called the Alexander Chest," she explained, "though *chest* makes it sound a lot bigger than it really is."

Just then, Lizzie spotted her parents. She waved to them and called, "Over here!"

Megan looked around. The other people in the lodge were relaxed, skiers on vacation taking their time and enjoying themselves. The Robinsons, on the other hand, were dashing over to them in business clothes, clearly in a hurry.

Chapter
Four

THE FAKE

I'm so glad you found a friend to ski with Lizzie," said Mona Robinson to her daughter. Lizzie looked a lot like her mother. They had the same sparkling blue eyes and the same blond hair.

"I'm Megan Ryder. It's nice to meet you," said Megan.

"Oh, you must be Erica Ryder's daughter. No wonder you're such a terrific skier," exclaimed Mrs. Robinson.

Uh-oh, thought Megan, I'd better be careful. She knew Erica Ryder was a famous skier who coached the Swiss women's ski team the year they won the Olympic gold medal. Megan was only about six then, but she remembered because their last names were the same and because her aunt always watched the winter Olympics.

"You could say that," Megan replied. Again, it wasn't a yes and it wasn't a no.

Paul Robinson, Lizzie's father, smiled at Lizzie and nodded when she told them how well the two of them had skied together. Megan got the feeling that he wasn't really listening.

"We just received a phone call from a London museum director," Mrs. Robinson said, her face flushed with excitement. "He's staying in a private home outside of the village. He heard about our purchase of the Alexander Chest and may be interested in acquiring it for the museum. Isn't it amazing how quickly word travels about something this important?"

"That's great!" cried Lizzie. "You buy it and sell it the same day."

"The director has asked us to dinner to discuss things," Mr. Robinson explained. "I know we promised to take you out for crêpes tonight—"

"Don't worry, Dad," interrupted Lizzie.

"Why don't the two of you go back to the suite and order room service?" suggested Mr. Robinson. "We have that cozy sitting area between our bedrooms, with a view of the mountains. Just sign the check with your name and the room number."

"Great idea," agreed Lizzie eagerly. "How about it, Megan? Do you think your mom will let you stay for dinner?"

"Thanks," Megan replied. "I was going to be by myself for dinner." She thought she sounded pretty convincing.

"So it's solved," declared Mrs. Robinson as she gave Lizzie a quick hug. She turned to her husband. "We'd better go, Paul."

"We'll arrange with the desk for a sitter from the hotel on our way out," said Mr. Robinson.

"A sitter? You mean a baby-sitter?" protested Lizzie. "We're too old for that. Back home, *we're* the baby-sitters."

"Back home is not a strange hotel in a foreign country." Mr. Robinson's tone was firm. "This is different. Besides, the sitter doesn't have to read you bedtime stories, you know." At that, he winked at the two of them.

"Oh, okay," agreed Lizzie. "But tell them not to send anybody right away. We want to check this place out before dinner."

"All right, you have an hour," said Mrs. Robinson. "It gets dark pretty early. Enjoy yourselves, girls." She and Mr. Robinson went to the front desk, and the girls headed for the Robinson's room to change.

Megan's feet were tired from skiing, and she gladly accepted Lizzie's offer to lend her a pair of après-ski boots. Ahh—they were so soft and comfortable! It took only a few minutes for the girls to decide that if the storm stopped, they would go sledding while it was still light enough. They could explore the rest of the lodge after dinner.

The snow had stopped falling and the wind had died down. The fourth time they whooshed down the sledding hill, sharp, loud barking startled Megan. She lost control and landed the sled in a snowbank. A husky pup came bounding through the snow, slid down the bank, and landed on the sled with a yelp.

"Oh, he's adorable!" cried Megan. The puppy instantly got up and leaped from Megan to Lizzie and back to Megan, his wet, pink tongue lapping at their cheeks. Megan checked his tag. MAXI, it said, along with the name of the lodge and village.

"We might have to have a baby-sitter later," said Lizzie. "But for now, we can 'baby-sit' Maxi." Megan laughed.

The girls giggled and squealed as they rolled in the snow with the puppy. For the next half hour, they had a

wonderful time taking him for sled rides. Every time they stopped, the puppy barked excitedly, making them tow him up the hill again and again. By the time the lodge owner whistled and Maxi went running off, both girls were exhausted and starving.

The baby-sitter was waiting in the suite when they arrived.

"Hello. I am Greta," said the woman, introducing herself in halting English. Greta looked like a skier. She was tall and muscular. Her thick auburn hair was pulled back with a black headband. Megan noticed that Greta limped slightly, putting her weight on her right leg.

"I fall," Greta tried to explain when she saw Megan watching her.

"You fell," said Megan politely. "Did you sprain your ankle?"

Greta nodded.

Lizzie and Megan were eager to order dinner from the room service menu. At first they thought the "American Special" of hamburgers and potato chips sounded good, but they decided to be daring and try French food. They offered to order something for Greta, but she told them she had already eaten.

"Two *saucissons en croûte*," Lizzie said into the phone. "One order of *pommes frites* and one order of *petits pois. Merci.*"

"What in the world are we having for dinner?" Megan wanted to know.

"Yummy sausage in a crust, fried potatoes, and peas," replied Lizzie, looking proud of herself. "I may not know the language, but we do go to a little French restaurant in our neighborhood for special occasions."

There was more food than Megan and Lizzie could finish. They offered some of the delicious *pommes frites* to Greta, but she didn't seem to have much of an appetite. She kept rubbing her sore ankle, her eyes constantly darting around the room.

"I guess her leg really hurts," Lizzie whispered to Megan when Greta wasn't listening.

"Well, something's sure bothering her," agreed Megan softly.

After dinner, the girls decided to visit Maxi before they had to go to bed. They told Greta they'd be back from the lobby in a few minutes.

"Greta looked happy to see us go," commented Lizzie.

"She's strange," Megan replied, but she headed down the stairs without thinking any more about her.

When Megan and Lizzie returned from playing with the puppy, Mr. and Mrs. Robinson were back at the suite. They looked very upset.

"What happened?" Lizzie asked right away.

"The dinner was a fake, a hoax. There was no such address, no such person," her mother explained breathlessly. "Something peculiar is going on."

"Where's the sitter?" asked Lizzie's father.

"She was right here when we left," Lizzie replied. "Her ankle was sprained. Maybe she decided to rest."

Without another word, Mr. Robinson dashed into their bedroom. "She's gone!" he shouted. "And so is the Alexander Chest!"

The Robinsons explained to the girls that when they tried to place the jeweled box in the safe at the front desk, the manager, a Monsieur Boucher, had told them that the hotel could not accept responsibility for such a valuable piece. He had suggested instead that they put the chest in a safe at the local bank when it opened in the morning. So the Robinsons had returned to the suite and had hidden the Alexander Chest in the deep blanket drawer in their room.

Lizzie turned to Megan, her face pale and her bottom lip quivering slightly. "Losing the Alexander Chest could cost my parents everything," she whispered. "And what if the thief had robbed them instead of just burglarizing the room? They might have been hurt."

Megan turned pale. A thief had been right here in this room, she thought. In fact . . . "What if it was Greta!" she whispered back to Lizzie. "How could Greta know the chest was here?"

Mr. Robinson was on the phone. ". . . get it back," he was saying.

Surely there was some way that Megan could help. But how?

Chapter Five

A SLEEPLESS NIGHT

The hotel security guard arrived right away. So did the local police. Soon the suite was filled with people examining the bedroom for clues and taking notes.

"I suspect this Greta, the baby-sitter, saw the jeweled box when you took it down to the safe," commented Chief Detective Court, head of the local police, in perfect English. "We have only recently been alerted to a ring of thieves making their way through the local ski resorts. They're famous for inside jobs like this one. I think we

have just had a taste of their cunning."

"We should never have left the girls or the Alexander Chest with a stranger," declared Mrs. Robinson.

"We're fine, Mom," said Lizzie. "But we shouldn't have let the sitter out of our sight."

"How in the world could you have suspected such a thing?" replied Mr. Robinson. "Though I do wish you girls had asked us whether you could leave the room to play."

Megan wondered if she looked as crestfallen as Lizzie did. The chest might be safe if they had just stayed put.

Monsieur Boucher arrived next and walked in nervous little circles around the room. Every once in awhile, he wiped beads of perspiration from his brow even though it wasn't especially hot in the room.

"What a terrible thing," he declared in a haughty tone. "Why, we have never known such dishonesty on the part of our staff."

Megan gave him a good hard look. His bulgy eyes reminded her of a fish she once caught and quickly threw back because it was so slimy and odd-looking. Something about his apology wasn't convincing.

"Do you have the address of your employee, Monsieur Boucher?" Detective Court wanted to know.

"An *imposteur*!" the manager cried. He explained that he had checked his files immediately and that the name and address the baby-sitter had given were phony.

"Somehow I don't trust Monsieur Boucher," Megan whispered to Lizzie.

"Funny, I was thinking the same thing," replied Lizzie.

When the police finally left, it was past ten o'clock.

"With all this activity, we forgot about our guest!" declared Mr. Robinson. "Megan, your mother must be worried sick. I owe her a personal apology."

"Oh, don't worry. I called her earlier," Megan said. She figured that they had been too distracted to notice she hadn't used the phone all night.

"I asked Megan to spend the night," said Lizzie. "I hope that's okay."

"Of course," said her mother. "You girls have been wonderful. And those feather beds look very inviting right about now."

Megan glanced into one of the bedrooms. The beds were carefully turned down, and she could see the puffy, pillowlike feather beds on top of the mattresses. You were supposed to lie down on the feather bed, and on top, a fluffy white comforter covered you. Megan was sure it would feel just like sleeping on a cloud.

Soon everyone said good night, went to their rooms, and closed the doors.

"I'm not tired," Lizzie protested. "It's five hours earlier back home."

"We could take a walk," suggested Megan. "You know, do our own little investigating . . ."

Lizzie liked that idea. They both knew they weren't supposed to go out without permission, but they were determined anyway. The closer they could get to solving this mystery, the better they both would feel and the happier everybody would be. Tiptoeing to the door, the girls slipped out. Downstairs, many lodge guests were still relaxing near a roaring fire, reading or chatting with one another, and sipping hot drinks. Outside the big front window, the snow was coming down hard again.

Megan spotted a large, potted evergreen tree in the lobby and motioned to Lizzie to hide with her behind it. There was a clear view of the front desk, of the EMPLOYEES ONLY sign on it—and, of Monsieur Boucher.

"Look!" whispered Lizzie, tapping Megan's shoulder. She pointed to two men and a woman, dressed in black turtlenecks and black ski pants, behind the desk. As the manager opened the hotel safe, their eyes nervously darted around the room.

"That's odd," whispered Megan. "None of the other hotel staff dresses that way."

"Maybe it's a robbery," Lizzie suggested in a low voice.

"It looks to me like they know each other," whispered Megan. "The manager doesn't seem very upset."

"Do you think they've stored something in the safe?" Lizzie asked.

"They look more like they'd be taking valuables out," said Megan. "I really don't think it's a robbery, but something is definitely going on."

Megan and Lizzie held their breath while Monsieur Boucher pulled the heavy safe door open and carefully removed something. It was wrapped in a white pillowcase, and seemed to be about the size of a small box. Without a word, the hotel manager handed it to one of the men, who tucked it under his arm.

"We should get the police back right now," whispered Lizzie in an angry voice.

"For what?" questioned Megan. "Because three people were given an object we can't identify out of the hotel safe? It wasn't a holdup. I don't think they'll rush over here for that."

"But we know what's going on," Lizzie went on, sounding frustrated. "We know that Greta stole the Alexander Chest and brought it down here to the manager and he put it in the safe."

"We *think* we know what's going on," Megan said calmly.

In every mystery book Megan had read, it was important to get enough facts to make an airtight case. You had to wait until you were certain. You had to collect clues, evidence, and witnesses. It was going to be up to her and Lizzie to find out for sure who the culprits were.

The three suspects dressed in black headed for the door. As they passed the potted tree where Megan and Lizzie were hiding, the girls backed into the shadows.

Then they followed a safe distance behind, into the freezing night.

The suspects headed for a small gray van parked near the lodge. They hesitated a moment, as though they had changed their minds about leaving. Then—luckily for Megan and Lizzie—they went only as far as the tavern next door to the lodge. Megan heard them murmur something about celebrating a little before they left town.

"What should we do?" groaned Lizzie. "They'll escape with the Alexander Chest."

"We'd better memorize the license plate number," replied Megan.

When the girls returned to the lodge, Monsieur Boucher was sipping a cup of coffee and talking on the phone. The girls crept closer.

"What do you mean that you can't find her? I need to speak with her right away," the hotel manager cried into the receiver, so angry that his voice carried halfway across the room. "Your neck is on the line." With that, he slammed down the phone and stormed out, leaving the desk unattended.

"Quick!" cried Megan. "We may only have a little time." With Lizzie following closely, Megan slipped behind the desk. She found a clean linen napkin on the counter. With one quick motion, she wrapped the coffee cup in the napkin and held it close to her.

"Let's go," she told Lizzie.

On the other side of the lobby, Megan spotted Chief Detective Court. He was rubbing his head, looking a bit puzzled.

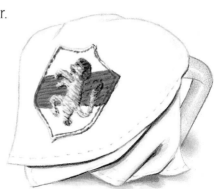

"Excuse me," said Megan. "We're—"

"You're the girls from the hotel suite," he said, interrupting her. "Isn't it a little late for you to be up?"

Megan wasn't certain that Detective Court would believe them when they told him their suspicions about Monsieur Boucher and the three people at the tavern. Besides, maybe he was a friend of the manager. Maybe even an accomplice. At this point, Megan wasn't willing to trust anyone.

So instead of telling Detective Court that the coffee cup in her hand belonged to Monsieur Boucher, she said, "I think the baby-sitter left this. If—when—you find the stolen jeweled box, the fingerprints on it should match the ones on the cup."

Carefully, Detective Court took the cup. "A good piece of detective work!" he exclaimed. "I'll take this over to the lab. Now you girls go back to your room. We don't need any more mysteries tonight. I'll take care of everything."

"There's one more thing," said Megan. "Lizzie and I thought we saw the baby-sitter driving a van when we were outside just a few minutes ago. I memorized the license plate." She told Detective Court the numbers.

"Why did you tell him that story about Greta?" Lizzie asked as they went back to their room.

"We're not sure of anything yet," Megan said. "But it can't hurt for Detective Court to know the suspicious license plate number, even if he thinks it's Greta's. If we're right, then at least the number can be traced."

Chapter
Six

GATHERING
EVIDENCE

Megan skied alone through a blinding snow in a race for her life. Just behind her, three figures followed her down the mountain, gaining on her at every turn. When she turned to look back, one of the figures raised his ski pole and pointed it in her direction. But it wasn't a ski pole. It was a gun. Suddenly, Megan saw the face of the person aiming right at her. It was none other than . . . Monsieur Boucher . . .

A loud knock awoke Megan from her bad dream. She

rubbed her eyes and listened as Lizzie's parents opened the door to the suite.

"*Bonjour*," came a voice filled with mock cheerfulness. It was Monsieur Boucher.

Megan wondered if there had been enough time for the police to identify the fingerprints on the cup. If they could find the Alexander Chest, they would have a case. If not, the person—or people—who had masterminded the theft would go free.

Megan and Lizzie dressed quickly. They agreed to grab a quick breakfast so they wouldn't have to waste any time getting back on the case.

"Ah, you girls are ready for a day on the slopes," said Monsieur Boucher when the two entered the sitting room. He moved aside and opened the door to the hallway, practically shoving them out.

"But . . ." stammered Lizzie.

"I think we forgot something," Megan started to say, wishing they had told Lizzie's parents everything when they returned to the room the night before. Now Megan had to think fast. She figured that if she pretended she had left something back in the room, she and Lizzie might get a second chance to talk to the Robinsons after the hotel manager had gone.

"You girls run along to breakfast," Mrs. Robinson said

wearily. Megan was sure she and Mr. Robinson had hardly slept a wink.

Monsieur Boucher smiled slyly. "Do run along. We have everything under control."

Sure, thought Megan. You mean *you* have everything under control.

"I'll only be a minute," Megan persisted, asking Lizzie to hold her mittens while she disappeared into the bathroom. Unfortunately, Monsieur Boucher was still there when she came out a short time later.

Before they went to breakfast, Megan and Lizzie checked out front for the van. It was gone, just as they had expected. But at least they had gotten the license plate number.

"What now?" asked Lizzie, finishing her eggs with a sigh. The frustration in her voice was unmistakable.

Megan looked at the plate of pastries, wondering how anybody could eat all the croissants and sweet rolls, no matter how good they were. Then she noticed a piece of white paper sticking out from a cherry roll on the bottom.

"Look," Megan exclaimed, wiping a bit of powdered sugar from the note.

"Read it!" cried Lizzie.

The note had been written with a soft dull pencil. Megan strained to see all the printed words. Then she read in a low voice:

> I *have something you need. It is not my fault. Come to the midway lodge now. Do not tell or we will all be in even more danger.*
>
> Greta

In order to get to the midway lodge, Megan and Lizzie had to take the gondola to the top of the mountain and ski down to it. At the top, they could see skiers racing down the slopes on the fresh powder. Little children fell over and over again on purpose and then screamed with delight.

Megan hoped it would be a good day for skiing. The slope looked terribly steep and difficult, much harder than the one she'd gone down the day before. She hoped it would be a good day for solving a mystery, too.

Megan and Lizzie put on their skis at the top and crossed the crest to a spot where they could pick one of four trails. Two of them were intermediate. The other two, marked with black diamonds, were for experts.

"I'm willing to try an expert trail with you," Lizzie said. "It'll be faster. But you might have to pull me out of the trees when I crash." Lizzie was obviously trying to make a joke, but Megan could tell that she was nervous.

Together the girls pushed off and headed down a trail called *Bonne Chance*—the trail sign also had the name in English: "Good Luck." Finally, they saw the lodge at the halfway point. Skiers could stop there to warm up, rest, and get something to eat or drink. The building, which looked more like a big cabin than a lodge, seemed to pop up on the horizon out of nowhere.

By the time Megan and Lizzie reached the lodge, their cheeks were red and their legs were tired.

"How are we going to find Greta?" Lizzie wanted to know.

"I have a feeling she'll find us," replied Megan. "I just hope she doesn't change her mind."

The girls were about to take off their skis when a woman opened the lodge door. It was a bright sunny day, almost windless, but the woman was wearing a wool ski mask.

"Weird," said Lizzie. "It's like spring today, and look at her."

The woman's heavy ski boots clomped loudly as she made her way down the cabin steps. She walked with a slight limp, definitely favoring one foot. The left one.

"Wait!" cried Megan. "There's something else. Watch her walk."

"Just like Greta, with the sprained ankle," said Lizzie.

After putting on her skis, the woman looked up and spotted Megan and Lizzie. She gave a slight jerk of her head in a "follow me" gesture. She led them behind the lodge.

"Okay, what's going on?" Megan asked Greta in the strongest voice she could muster. She thought it was important to sound brave and convincing when you were dealing with criminals.

"We know you took the chest from my parents' room!" cried Lizzie.

Greta pulled off her mask. She looked more terrified than wicked. "I meet three people in the village one night who say they have job for me. They say I will be paid very well."

"Who were they?" asked Lizzie

"Who paid you?" demanded Megan.

"They take me to the man at the desk at that fancy lodge. He tells me it is a small thing and not so bad to do. Then he promises he gives me work, a job as waitress, with good regular pay, too, after I get the chest for him."

"Monsieur Boucher," said Megan. "We were right. So why are you coming to us now?"

"I give him that chest, but the man refuses me the pay and refuses me the waitress job. I leave, but before I go, I tell to him that I will"—Greta struggled for the right words—"I will . . . spill the beans. I think I am in deep over my head. Your parents can maybe say a good word with the police for me." Greta's voice was shaky, and her hands trembled as she held them out toward Lizzie. The woman seemed very frightened. "And there is something you do not know." She paused again, then continued. "The three are looking for me."

"Why would they be interested in you now? You did your job. They're finished with you, unless they're worried about you spilling the beans, too. But I don't think that's a problem," said Megan. "They'll figure you're too scared of being put in jail."

"You do not understand," Greta protested as she played with the strap on her mittens. "*Oui*, I did my job, as you say. But I am angry. So I take the little chest back from them last night at the tavern while they celebrate. And now—"

"And now they're after you." Megan finished the sentence for Greta. "You've probably been followed. Criminals like that are very clever."

Suddenly Greta's face filled with terror. Her mouth flew open and she looked as though she'd seen a ghost. The girls turned and saw the three skiers in black parkas and ski pants schussing toward the cabin—and toward the three of them. They had probably been looking for Greta all over the slopes, and they had finally found her.

Greta pulled something from her parka. It was in a white pillowcase. "They do not want me," she said. She tossed the object to Megan. "They are after the little chest."

Ignoring her sprained ankle, Greta pushed Megan and Lizzie out of the way and skied toward a trail called *Dernière Chance* —"Last Chance," according to the sign—to make her escape. Before she disappeared from view, Greta shouted back to Megan and Lizzie: "Ski for your lives!"

Chapter Seven

FLYING DOWN THE MOUNTAIN

Quick! Go to the gondola station and phone Detective Court for help," cried Megan. "Now that we're sure, you can explain everything. He'll know what to do. Then take the gondola to the bottom. It'll be faster that way."

Megan pointed to the gondola station at the mountain's midpoint where weary skiers could ride the rest of the way down. She unzipped her parka enough to tuck the Alexander Chest deep down inside, then zipped

it up quickly, knowing the jeweled box was safe—for
the time being.

"What will you do?" Lizzie demanded. "They must
have seen you take the chest from Greta."

"Don't worry. I've got it all figured out. I'll take *La
Montagne du Diable*—'The Devil's Mountain'—to the
bottom. It's the fastest trail, and the hardest. Maybe I
can lose them."

"Not that trail!" shrieked Lizzie. "There's a warning
at the base that you take it at your own risk. And the
trail has been even tougher since the avalanche earlier
this winter."

Megan took a deep breath. So far, she hadn't had
time to be afraid. With so much happening and so much
at stake, she'd been brave and clever in the face of real
danger. Now, for the first time, came a true test on the
mountain. The weather could change in a flash, or there
could be ice—even avalanches—on such difficult trails.
Still, she knew what had to be done.

"There's no time to argue," Megan declared. "Now go!
I'll be okay."

Lizzie headed toward the gondola, and Megan turned
straight down the most dangerous trail on the mountain.
She felt the sun on her back and the wind in her face as
she pushed off. When she looked back, she saw three

people in black. They were closing fast. Megan knew that one slip, one wrong turn, and it was all over. . . .

Although Megan skied like the wind, one of the skiers was even faster. But when she turned sharply, he veered wildly off the trail and into the woods. So much for his skills on an expert trail, thought Megan gleefully.

A field of icy moguls—small rocklike bumps on the trail, one right after the other—was just ahead. It looked like some kind of impossible obstacle course. Megan kept her knees relaxed as she bounced up and down over the tops of the moguls. She was sure she'd lose one of the two remaining skiers, but they were only slowed down.

Megan felt to make sure the Alexander Chest was still secure, then went full speed ahead. She was amazed how steady and balanced she felt. She knew she wouldn't fall. The trees on the sides of the trail, encrusted with snow, flew by so quickly that it was like watching a movie in fast-forward. Megan took a deep breath. The clear clean air smelled of pine trees, but there was no time to enjoy the day or the scenery. The two remaining thieves were quickly gaining on her.

As the trail narrowed, Megan glanced back. Both skiers were closing fast. When she turned around again, she could see all the way to the bottom of the run. And she could spot a group of people waiting there. She wasn't sure, but she thought one of them was Detective Court, with Lizzie standing beside him.

Please let the plan work, thought Megan. It may be our only chance!

With her skis close together, Megan headed for the fall line—the straightest and steepest way down, it was the final run where only the experts dared to get up the kind of speed that was needed to pull off the plan. Just ahead, the trail was narrow and lined on both sides with trees. Megan inhaled sharply. The sign said this part of the trail was called *La Rue de l'Hôpital*—"Hospital Street"!

I want the thieves to be watching me, Megan thought as she sped down at breakneck speed. And they were close behind, staring right at her and doing exactly as she hoped they would.

At the bottom of the mountain, Lizzie was madly waving her red ski hat, a signal she and Megan had agreed upon, and pointing to a thick grove of trees just a few yards ahead of Megan.

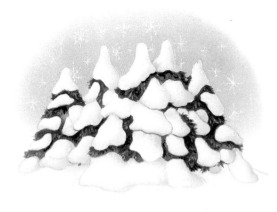

Megan crouched even lower, putting her body into a tight tuck. As she flew past the trees, she saw police officers on both sides. She chanced a peek back over her shoulder. The trap!

A rope was stretched tight across the trail. As the thieves hit it, they were knocked flat. Their poles went flying and their skis were scattered on the slope.

Megan practically screeched to a stop, spraying snow in a rainbow arc yards wide.

"You were great!" cried Lizzie, rushing up to Megan. "They didn't know what hit them."

It suddenly seemed that police were everywhere, arresting the startled thieves and taking them off to jail. Detective Court had everything under control.

"One of them went off the trail into the woods!" cried Megan, afraid that the thief would escape.

"Don't worry," replied Lizzie. "I heard the police radio report. The ski patrol is taking him down the mountain on a stretcher. The only place he's going is a hospital with a broken leg. He can rest up in jail."

Lizzie's parents came running across the snow. They were wearing ski clothes like everybody else, and Megan hardly recognized them.

"Monsieur Boucher is in custody for questioning," Mrs. Robinson told them breathlessly. "And Greta turned herself in. She told the police everything."

"How did you find out about Monsieur Boucher?" Lizzie asked her parents.

"Why, the note in soap on the bathroom mirror," Mr. Robinson replied. "Megan, you wrote that while Monsieur Boucher insisted on hanging around our suite, didn't you?" Megan blushed as she nodded. "Thanks to you, we were able to keep an eye on Monsieur Boucher until he was arrested. That was very clever of you, Megan. You really ought to be a detective."

Megan smiled. Or a mystery writer, she said to herself.

"Hey, aren't you forgetting something?" Lizzie teased, patting the front of Megan's parka.

Megan felt something hard against her. The Alexander Chest was still tucked inside, safe and sound. "I did almost forget," she cried. "Here." With great care, she handed the box in the pillowcase to Detective Court. "I think you'll find that the fingerprints on the chest match the fingerprints on Monsieur Boucher's coffee mug."

"Monsieur Boucher's cup?" Detective Court asked. "But you said—"

"It's a little complicated," said Megan. "But yes, it's definitely his."

"Good work!" the detective congratulated her. "We traced the license plate, too. These seem to be the same people who have been hitting other resorts. Your quick thinking saved us a lot of time." He took the pillowcase off the precious chest.

The jewels on the box glittered in the bright sunlight. The diamond that Lizzie had described was not really blue, like the blue of the sky. It was more incredible than that—an icy blue that looked like a high mountain peak on a crystal-clear day.

"I'll say it again, Megan. You were great!" declared Lizzie. "You're just about the bravest person I know."

"Thanks," replied Megan. She had to admit that she felt really good about the way things had turned out.

As they headed back to the lodge, Lizzie invited Megan for another cup of hot chocolate to celebrate.

"Thanks, Lizzie, but it's time for me to go home. "What Megan was really thinking was: It's time for *my* vacation now, with my dad!

Megan said good-bye to the Robinsons in the lobby of the lodge. The room was filled with people tramping around in their big ski boots. The fire in the fireplace was blazing. Everybody was friendly and relaxed and having a good time.

Megan stopped at a tall mirror near the stairs. When she looked into it, she saw how rosy her cheeks were and how healthy she looked. She smiled at herself.

Then the next thing Megan knew, she was back in Ellie's attic, standing in front of the long gilt-edged mirror. And her nose was still frosty.

Chapter
Eight

SAFE AND SOUND

O n the plane to Paris, Megan got to sit by the window. The Jamisons said she'd get a better view of the lights of Paris that way. As they circled the city in preparation for landing, Megan felt like a bird soaring high above a fantasy land. The lights of the city seemed to twinkle at her. "*Bonjour, Paris,*" she whispered. "Hello, Paris."

The plane to Switzerland wasn't as small as she had feared. The attendants made a big fuss about her

Svizzera
Switzerland

traveling alone. They let Megan sit in the first row, and taught her how to say "Where can I buy pizza?" and "Please direct me to the nearest bathroom" in French. Flying alone turned out to be really fun.

The plane did fly low, but that gave Megan a chance to see mountain scenery so breathtaking that she knew she would never forget the sight. It was early morning when they landed at the small airport near the resort in the Alps. As Megan gathered up her backpack and her books, she pictured her father's welcoming smile.

"Megan! Megan!" a man shouted as she walked through the gate. She would know that voice anywhere!

"Dad!" cried Megan, jumping into her father's arms for a big hug.

"How was the trip?" her father asked. "Did everything go okay?" He wrinkled his brow and looked concerned.

"Everything was great," She replied. Then she showed him the small silver airplane pin that one of the flight attendants had given her.

"That ought to look good on a new parka," her father said. "You've practically outgrown the one you're wearing. How about it?"

"A new parka!" exclaimed Megan, thinking of the gold parka from the attic. Maybe they could find one just like it.

The resort village looked so much like the one in her adventure that Megan couldn't believe her eyes. The lodge looked familiar, too, except that it was more like a French chalet, with small iron balconies overlooking the mountainside. She and her father had adjoining rooms, with a bathroom between them that they would share.

"I've really been looking forward to this," said Megan's father as he helped her unpack.

"Me, too," replied Megan. "But I almost got cold

feet," she admitted. "You know, about traveling alone and being in a foreign country."

"I sometimes feel the same way," admitted Megan's father as he took her hand.

"But you've traveled all over the world!" exclaimed Megan, surprised that her father would be nervous about anything like that.

"Sure," he replied. "I love my work and all the exciting places I go, but everyone gets the jitters every now and then."

"Are you worried about skiing?" Megan wanted to know.

"Not with you here," her father kidded. "Now I have somebody to pick me up and dust off the snow!"

At the bottom of her suitcase, Megan found a note from her mother. She was always tucking surprise notes in secret places where Megan would eventually find them. The note said:

> By the time you read this, you will have become a
> world traveler! Have a great time with your dad.
> > Love, Mom
> P.S: I love you and miss you already, honey bunny.

"Mom said we're snow bunnies," Megan told her father as they headed downstairs for breakfast the next day.

"Well, we'll be the bravest bunnies on the slopes,"

declared her father as they ordered a big breakfast of omelettes with mushrooms and hot, flaky croissants. "I've signed us up for a ski class," he told her. "Everybody has to start somewhere."

Before their first class, Megan and her father did some shopping. Megan didn't find the exact same parka that she'd worn on her adventure, but she did find a bright yellow one with a hat to match.

"Now you look like an expert!" Her father made the thumbs-up sign. "Let's find our class."

By the end of the first lesson, Megan and her father were skiing down the beginner's slope without falling down. They had learned to snowplow, to turn, and to stop quickly. Megan laughed to herself when she thought back to the expert trails she had schussed down on her mirror adventure.

"Not bad for bunnies," joked her father.

Skiing wasn't the only thing to do at the resort. In fact, there were so many activities to choose from that Megan worried they wouldn't have time to do everything in just one week. As she and her father walked through the village, most of the people seemed to be heading to some special event. "Let's see what's going on," her father suggested. "We may be in for a treat."

He was right. A curling contest was taking place right

there in the village. They watched as two teams of four people each slid something called a curling stone across the ice toward a target in the center. It was a little like ice hockey and very competitive. Megan wondered if her friends back home might like to learn the game. It looked like fun.

"I bet curling is hard to learn," she told her father.

"So what if it is?" he replied. "I know you can do anything you put your mind to."

"It's hard sometimes . . ." Megan began.

"Sure it is," said her father. "Once, when I was your age, I had a chance to go on a camping trip for a week with my best friends. I said I would go. We were all so excited. Then I chickened out at the last minute."

"But why?"

"Well, I wasn't much of a swimmer yet. In fact, I was afraid of water. And I was afraid to let my friends know. So I missed out on one of the greatest camping trips of all time. At least according to my friends."

Megan laughed, and her father put his arm around her. "Sometimes courage means being able to admit that you're scared."

Before dinner, Megan and her father decided to go sledding on the hill behind the hotel. The snow was tightly packed there and just right for a fast run.

The hotel had
sleds of all sizes
lined up against
a wall for
the guests.

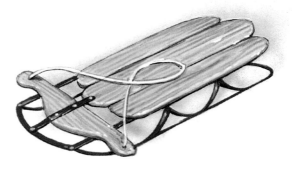

The two of
them practically
flew down the hill.
Just the way the
air smelled and
the trees looked
reminded Megan of her adventure. She was glad she'd
had that time to get ready for this trip with her father.

Before Megan turned off the light at bedtime that
night, she wrote five postcards: three to her friends, one
to her mother with a P.S. to Aunt Frances, and one to
Ellie. Ellie's card had a wintry Alps scene on the front.
When she closed her eyes, Megan could almost see Ellie
pasting the postcard in her album.

Diary

Dear Diary,

I feel like a world traveler now! Boarding the plane to come home felt so different from that flight going over. I knew how to find the right seat, what all the buttons on my armrest meant, and where to find the extra pillows and blankets (they're in the storage bin above your head). Flying really is fun, and learning a new language is not so hard. Sometimes people would see me struggling with my dictionary, trying to figure out a word or a phrase and they'd offer to help me out. I met a lot of people when I was trying to say things like, "How much are the postcards?" and "I'll have a hamburger with everything on it." I think I'll take French in school next year. Then I'll be able to read books in two languages.

There was so much to tell Keisha, Heather, and

Alison when I got back. I started with my ski

adventure in the attic. My friends couldn't believe

that I had actually solved a crime. They all agreed

that I should write a mystery. Ellie wanted to know

about the Alps. She had already put my postcard in

her album. Maybe I'll start my own album. By the

way, Diary, I'm sorry I left you home. I knew there

just wouldn't be a lot of time for writing in you. But

I did miss you! And now I can make up for lost time.

   I might not be an expert skier now, like in the

adventure, but I have to admit that I'm pretty good.

After awhile I wasn't worrying about falling down.

In fact, Dad and I were skiing the intermediate

slopes by the time the week was over. Once we

even took part of an expert slope, just to try it out.

I told Dad he had a lot of potential.

   I've done a lot of thinking about courage and

what it really means to me. I think it meant being brave about leaving home for the very first time. During the adventure, there were times when I guess I just wanted my mother to come to my rescue. But I knew she'd want me to use my head, so I tried hard to take care of myself. And I did, plus helping some people out.

Love,

Megan